James Matthew Barrie

An Edinburgh Eleven

Pencil portraits from college life

James Matthew Barrie

An Edinburgh Eleven
Pencil portraits from college life

ISBN/EAN: 9783337427207

Printed in Europe, USA, Canada, Australia, Japan

Cover: Foto ©Andreas Hilbeck / pixelio.de

More available books at **www.hansebooks.com**

AN EDINBURGH ELEVEN.

Pencil Portraits from College Life.

BY

J. M. BARRIE,

AUTHOR OF "WHEN A MAN'S SINGLE," "AULD LICHT IDYLLS," ETC.

LONDON:

OFFICE OF THE "BRITISH WEEKLY,"

27, PATERNOSTER ROW.

MDCCCLXXXIX.

CONTENTS.

LORD ROSEBERY.

THE first time I ever saw Lord Rosebery was in Edinburgh when I was a student, and I flung a clod of earth at him. He was a peer; those were my politics.

I missed him, and I have heard a good many journalists say since then that he is a difficult man to hit. One who began by liking him and is now scornful, which is just the reverse process from mine, told me the reason why. He had some brochures to write on the Liberal leaders, and got on nicely till he reached Lord Rosebery, where he stuck. In vain he walked round his lordship, looking for an opening. The man was naturally indignant; he is the father of a family.

Lord Rosebery is forty-one years of age, and has missed many opportunities of becoming the bosom friend of Lord Randolph

Churchill. They were at Eton together and at Oxford, and have met since. As a boy the Liberal played at horses, and the Tory at running off with other boys' caps. Lord Randolph was the more distinguished at the University. One day a proctor ran him down in the streets smoking in his cap and gown. The undergraduate remarked on the changeability of the weather, but the proctor, gasping at such bravado, demanded his name and college. Lord Randolph failed to turn up next day at St. Edmund Hall to be lectured, but strolled to the proctor's house about dinner-time. " Does a fellow, name of Moore, live here ? " he asked. The footman contrived not to faint. " He do," he replied, severely ; "but he are at dinner." " Ah ! take him in my card," said the unabashed caller. The Merton books tell that for this the noble lord was fined ten pounds.

There was a time when Lord Rosebery would have reformed the House of Lords to a site nearer Newmarket. As politics took a firmer grip of him, it was Newmarket that seemed a long way off. One day at Edinburgh he realized the disadvantage of owning swift horses. His brougham had met him at Waverley Station to take him to Dalmeny. Lord Rosebery opened the door of the carriage to put in some papers, and then turned away. The coachman, too well bred to look round, heard the door shut, and thinking that his master was inside, set off at once. Pursuit was attempted, but what was there in Edinburgh streets to make up on those horses? The coachman drove seven miles, until he reached a point in the Dalmeny parks where it was his lordship's custom to alight and open a gate. Here the brougham stood for some minutes, awaiting Lord Rosebery's convenience. At last the coachman became uneasy and dismounted. His brain reeled when he saw an empty brougham. He could have sworn to seeing his lordship enter. There were his papers. What had happened? With a quaking hand the horses were turned, and, driving back, the coachman looked fearfully along the sides of the road. He met Lord Rosebery travelling in great good humour by the luggage omnibus.

Whatever is to be Lord Rosebery's future, he has reached that stage in a statesman's career when his opponents cease to question his capacity. His speeches showed him long ago a man of brilliant parts. His tenure of the Foreign Office proved him heavy metal. Were the Gladstonians to return to power, the other Cabinet posts might go anywhere, but the Foreign Secretary is arranged for. Where his predecessors had clouded their meaning in words till it was as wrapped up as a Mussulman's head, Lord Rosebery's were the straightforward dispatches of a man with his mind made up. German influence was spoken of; Count Herbert Bismarck had been seen shooting Lord Rosebery's partridges. This was the evidence: there has never been any other, except that German methods commended themselves to the Minister rather than those of France. His relations with the French Government were cordial. "The talk of Bismarck's shadow behind Rosebery," a great French politician said lately, "I put aside with a smile; but how about the Jews?" Probably few persons realize what a power the

Jews are in Europe, and in Lord Rosebery's position he is a strong man if he holds his own with them. Any fears on that ground have, I should say, been laid by his record at the Foreign Office.

Lord Rosebery had once a conversation with Prince Bismarck, to which, owing to some oversight, the Paris correspondent of the *Times* was not invited. M. Blowitz only smiled good-naturedly, and of course his report of the proceedings appeared all the same. Some time afterwards Lord Rosebery was introduced to this remarkable man, who, as is well known, carries Cabinet appointments in his pocket, and complimented him on his report. "Ah, it was all right, was it?" asked Blowitz, beaming. Lord Rosebery explained that any fault it had was that it was all wrong. "Then if Bismarck did not say that to you," said Blowitz, regally, "I know he intended to say it."

The " Uncrowned King of Scotland " is a title that has been made for Lord Rosebery, whose country has had faith in him from the beginning. Mr. Gladstone is the only other

man who can make so many Scotsmen take
politics as if it were the Highland Fling.
Once when Lord Rosebery was firing an
Edinburgh audience to the delirium point,
an old man in the hall shouted out, " I dinna
hear a word he says, but it's grand, it's
grand ! " During the first Midlothian cam-
paign Mr. Gladstone and Lord Rosebery were
the father and son of the Scottish people.
Lord Rosebery rode into fame on the top of
that wave, and he has kept his place in the
hearts of the people, and in oleographs on
their walls, ever since. In all Scottish matters
he has the enthusiasm of a Burns dinner, and
his humour enables him to pay compliments.
When he says agreeable things to Scotsmen
about their country, there is a twinkle in his
eye and in theirs to which English scribes cannot give a meaning. He has unveiled so many
Burns' statues that an American lecturess
explains, " Curious thing, but I feel somehow
I am connected with Lord Rosebery. I go
to a place and deliver a lecture on Burns ;
they collect subscriptions for a statue, and he
unveils it." Such is the delight of the Scottish

students in Lord Rosebery, that he may be
said to have made the triumphal tour of the
northern universities as their Lord Rector ;
he lost the post in Glasgow lately through a
quibble, but had the honour with the votes.
His address to the Edinburgh undergraduates
on " Patriotism " was the best thing he ever
did outside politics, and made the students his
for life. Some of them had smuggled into the
hall a chair with " Gaelic chair " placarded on
it, and the Lord Rector unwittingly played
into their hands. In a noble peroration he
exhorted his hearers to high aims in life.
" Raise your country," he exclaimed (cheers) ;
" raise yourselves (renewed cheering) ; raise
your university " (thunders of applause).
From the back of the hall came a solemn
voice, " Raise the chair ! " Up went the Gaelic
chair.

Even Lord Rosebery's views on Imperial
Federation can become a compliment to
Scotland. Having been all over the world
himself, and felt how he grew on his travels,
Lord Rosebery maintains that every British
statesman should visit India and the Colonies.

He said that first at a semi-public dinner in the country—and here I may mention that on such occasions he has begun his speeches less frequently than any other prominent politician with a statement that others could be got to discharge the duty better; in other words, he has several times omitted this introduction. On his return to London he was told that his colleagues in the Administration had been seeing how his scheme would work out. "We found that if your rule were enforced, the Cabinet would consist of yourself and Childers." "This would be an ideal Cabinet," Lord Rosebery subsequently remarked in Edinburgh, "for it would be entirely Scottish"; Mr. Childers being member for a Scottish constituency.

The present unhappy division of the Liberal party has made enemies of friends for no leading man so little as for Lord Rosebery. There are forces working against him, no doubt, in comparatively high places, but the Unionists have kept their respect for him. His views may be wrong, but he is about the only Liberal leader, with the noble exception of Lord Hartington, of whom troublous times have not rasped the temper. Though a great reader, he is not a literary man like Mr. Morley, who would, however, be making phrases where Lord Rosebery would make laws. Sir William Harcourt has been spoken of as a possible Prime Minister, but surely it will never come to that. If Mr. Gladstone's successor is chosen from those who have followed him on the Home Rule question, he probably was not rash in himself naming Lord Rosebery.

Lord Rosebery could not now step up without stepping into the Premiership. His humour, which is his most obvious faculty, has been a prop to him many a time ere now, but, if I was his adviser, I should tell him that it has served its purpose. There are a great many excellent people who shake their heads over it in a man who has become a power in the land. "Let us be grave," said Dr. Johnson once to a merry companion, "for here comes a fool." In an unknown novel there is a character who says of himself that "he is not stupid enough ever to be a great man."

I happen to know that this reflection was evolved by the author out of thinking over Lord Rosebery. It is not easy for a bright man to be heavy, and Lord Rosebery's humour is so spontaneous that if a joke is made in their company he has always finished laughing before Lord Hartington begins. Perhaps when Lord Rosebery is on the point of letting his humour run off with him in a public speech he could recover his solemnity by thinking of the *Examiner*.

PROFESSOR MASSON.

THOUGH a man might, to my mind, be better employed than in going to college, it is his own fault if he does not strike on some one there who sends his life off at a new angle. If, as I take it, the glory of a professor is to give elastic minds their proper bent, Masson is a name his country will retain a grip of. There are men who are good to think of, and as a rule we only know them from their books. Something of our pride in life would go with their fall. To have one such professor at a time is the most a university can hope of human nature, so Edinburgh need not expect another just yet. These, of course, are only to be taken as the reminiscences of a student. I seem to remember everything Masson said, and the way he said it.

Having immediately before taken lodgings

in a crow's nest, my first sight of Masson was specially impressive. It was the opening of the session, when fees were paid, and a whisper ran round the quadrangle that Masson had set off home with three hundred one-pound notes stuffed into his trouser pockets. There was a solemn swell of awestruck students to the gates, and some of us could not help following him. He took his pockets coolly. When he stopped it was at a second-hand bookstall, where he rummaged for a long time. Eventually he pounced upon a dusty, draggled little volume, and went off proudly with it beneath his arm. He seemed to look suspiciously at strangers now, but it was not the money but the book he was keeping guard over. His pockets, however, were unmistakably bulging out. I resolved to go in for literature.

Masson, however, always comes to my memory first knocking nails into his desk or trying to tear the gas-bracket from its socket. He said that the Danes scattered over England, taking such a hold as a nail takes when it is driven into wood. For the moment he saw his desk turned into England ; he whirled an

invisible hammer in the air, and down it
came on the desk with a crash. No one who
has sat under Masson can forget how the
Danes nailed themselves upon England. His
desk is thick with their tombstones. It was
when his mind groped for an image that he
clutched the bracket. He seemed to tear his
good things out of it. Silence overcame the
class. Some were fascinated by the man ;
others trembled for the bracket. It shook,
groaned, and yielded. Masson said another
of the things that made his lectures literature ;
the crisis was passed ; and everybody breathed
again.

He masters a subject by letting it master
him ; for though his critical reputation is built
on honesty, it is his enthusiasm that makes
his work warm with life. Sometimes he
entered the classroom so full of what he had
to say that he began before he reached his
desk. If he was in the middle of a peroration when the bell rang, even the back-benches
forgot to empty. There were the inevitable
students to whom literature is a trial, and
sometimes they call attention to their suffer-

ings by a scraping of the feet. Then the professor tried to fix his eyeglass on them, and when it worked properly they were transfixed. As a rule, however, it required so many adjustments that by the time his eye took hold of it he had remembered that students were made so, and his indignation went. Then, with the light in his eye that some photographer ought to catch, he would hope that his lecture was not disturbing their conversation. It was characteristic of his passion for being just that when he had criticised some writer severely he would remember that the back-benches could not understand that criticism and admiration might go together, unless they were told so again.

The test of a sensitive man is that he is careful of wounding the feelings of others. Once, I remember, a student was reading a passage aloud, assuming at the same time such an attitude that the Professor could not help remarking that he looked like a teapot. It was exactly what he did look like, and the class applauded. But next moment Masson had apologized for being personal. Such

reminiscences are what make the old literature classroom to thousands of graduates a
delight to think of.

When the news of Carlyle's death reached
the room, Masson could not go on with his
lecture. Every one knows what Carlyle has
said of him ; and no one who has heard it
will ever forget what he has said of Carlyle.
Here were two men who understood each
other. One of the Carlylean pictures one
loves to dwell on shows them smoking together, with nothing breaking the pauses but
Mrs. Carlyle's needles. Carlyle told Masson
how he gave up smoking and then took to it
again. He had walked from Dumfriesshire
to Edinburgh to consult a doctor about his
health, and was advised to lose his pipe. He
smoked no more, but his health did not im-
prove, and then one day he walked in a wood.
At the foot of a tree lay a pipe, a tobacco
pouch, a match-box. He saw clearly that
this was a case of Providential interference,
and from that moment he smoked again.
There the Professor's story stops. I have no
doubt, though, that he nodded his head when

Carlyle explained what the pipe and tobacco were doing there. Masson's " Milton " is, of course, his great work, but for sympathetic analysis I know nothing to surpass his " Chatterton." Lecturing on Chatterton one day, he remarked, with a slight hesitation, that had the poet mixed a little more in company and—and smoked, his morbidness would not have poisoned him. That turned my thoughts to smoking, because I meant to be a Chatterton, but greater. Since then the professor has warned me against smoking too much. He was smoking at the time.

This is no place to follow Masson's career, nor to discuss his work. To reach his position one ought to know his definition of a man-of-letters. It is curious, and, like most of his departures from the generally accepted, sticks to the memory. By a man-of-letters he does not mean the poet, for instance, who is all soul, so much as the strong-brained writer whose guardian angel is a fine sanity. He used to mention John Skelton, the Wolsey satirist, and Sir David Lindsay, as typical men-of-letters from this point of view, and it is as a man-of-letters of that class that Masson is best considered. In an age of many whipper-snappers in criticism he is something of a Gulliver.

The students in that class liked to see their professor as well as hear him. I let my hair grow long because it only annoyed other people, and one day there was dropped into my hand a note containing sixpence and the words: "The students sitting behind you present their compliments, and beg that you will get your hair cut with the enclosed, as it interferes with their view of the professor."

Masson, when he edited "Macmillan's," had all the best men round him. His talk of Thackeray is specially interesting, but he always holds that in conversation Douglas Jerrold was unapproachable. Jerrold told him a good story of his sea-faring days. His ship was lying off Gibraltar, and for some hours Jerrold, though only a midshipman, was left in charge. Some of the sailors begged to get ashore, and he let them, on the promise that they would bring him back some oranges. One of them disappeared, and the midshipman suffered for it. More than twenty years afterwards Jerrold was looking in at a window in the Strand when he seemed to know the face of a weather-beaten man who was doing the same thing. Suddenly he remembered, and put his hand on the other's shoulder. "My man," he said, "you have been a long time with those oranges!" The sailor recognized him, turned white, and took to his heels. There is, too, the story of how Dickens and Jerrold made up their quarrel at the Garrick Club. It was the occasion on which Masson first met the author of "Pickwick." Dickens and Jerrold had not spoken for a year, and they both happened to have friends at dinner in the strangers' room, Masson being Jerrold's guest. The two hosts sat back to back, but did not address each other, though the conversation was general. At last Jerrold could stand it no longer. Turning, he exclaimed, "Charley, my boy, how are you?" Dickens wheeled round and grasped his hand.

Many persons must have noticed that, in appearance, Masson is becoming more and more like Carlyle every year. How would

you account for it ? It is a thing his old
students often discuss when they meet, espe-
cially those of them who, when at college,
made up their minds to dedicate their first
book to him. The reason they seldom do it
is because the book does not seem good
enough.

III

PROFESSOR JOHN STUART BLACKIE.

LATELY I was told that Blackie—one does not say Mr. Cromwell—is no longer Professor of Greek in Edinburgh University. What nonsense some people talk. As if Blackie were not part of the building. In his class one day he spoke touchingly of the time when he would have to join Socrates in the Elysian fields. A student cheered—no one knows why. "It won't be for some time yet," added John Stuart.

Blackie takes his ease at home in a dressing-gown and straw hat. This shows that his plaid really does come off. "My occupation nowadays," he said to me recently, "is business, blethers, bothers, beggars, and backgammon." He has also started a profession of going to public meetings, and hurrying home to write letters to the newspapers about them. When the editor shakes the manuscript a sonnet falls out.   I think I remember the Professor's saying that he had never made five shillings by his verses.   To my mind they are worth more than that.

Though he has explained them frequently, there is still confusion about Blackie's politics. At Manchester they thought he was a Tory, and invited him to address them on that understanding.   " I fancy I astonished them," the Professor said to me.   This is quite possible.   Then he was mistaken for a Liberal.

The fact is that Blackie is a philosopher who follows the golden mean.   He sees this himself.   A philosopher who follows the golden mean is thus a man who runs zig-zag between two extremes.   You will observe that he who does this is some time before he arrives anywhere.

The Professor has said that he has the strongest lungs in Scotland.   Of the many compliments that might well be paid him, not the least worthy would be this, that he is as healthy mentally as physically.   Mrs. Norton begins a novel with the remark that one of the finest sights conceivable is a well-preserved gentleman of middle-age.   It will be some time yet before Blackie reaches middle-age, but there must be something wrong with you if you can look at him without feeling refreshed.   Did you ever watch him marching along Princes Street on a warm day, when every other person was broiling in the sun? His head is well thrown back, the staff, grasped in the middle, jerks back and forward like a weaver's shuttle, and the plaid flies in the breeze.   Other people's clothes are hanging limp.   Blackie carries his breeze with him.

A year or two ago Mr. Gladstone, when at Dalmeny, pointed out that he had the advantage over Blackie in being of both Highland and Lowland extraction.   The Professor, however, is as Scotch as the thistle or his native hills, and Mr. Gladstone, quite justifiably, considers him the most outstanding of living Scotsmen.   Blackie is not quite sure himself.   Not long ago I heard him read a preface to a life of Mr. Gladstone that was being printed at Smyrna in modern Greek.   He told his readers to remember that Mr. Gladstone was a great scholar and an upright statesman. They would find it easy to do this if they first remembered that he was Scottish.

The *World* included Blackie in its list of "Celebrities at Home." It said that the door was opened by a red-headed lassie. That was probably meant for local colour, and it amused every one who knew Mrs. Blackie. The Professor is one of the most genial of men, and will show you to your room himself, talking six languages. This tends to make the conversation one-sided, but he does not mind that. He still writes a good deal, spending several hours in his library daily, and his talk is as brilliant as ever. His writing nowadays is less sustained than it was, and he prefers flitting from one subject to another to evolving a great work. When he dips his pen into an ink-pot it at once writes a sonnet—so strong is the force of habit. Recently he wrote a page about Carlyle in a little book issued by the Edinburgh students' bazaar committee. In this he reproved Carlyle for having "bias."

Blackie wonders why people should have bias.

Some readers of this may in their student days have been invited to the Greek professor's house to breakfast without knowing why they were selected from among so many. It was not, as they are probably aware, because of their classical attainments, for they were too thoughtful to be in the prize-list; nor was it because of the charm of their manners or the fascination of their conversation. When the Professor noticed any physical peculiarity about a student, such as a lisp, or a glass eye, or one leg longer than the other, or a broken nose, he was at once struck by it, and asked him to breakfast. They were very lively breakfasts, the eggs being served in tureens; but sometimes it was a collection of the maimed and crooked, and one person at the table—not the host himself—used to tremble lest, making mirrors of each other, the guests should see why they were invited.

Sometimes, instead of asking a student to breakfast, Blackie would instruct another student to request his company to tea. Then the two students were told to talk about paulo-post futures in the cool of the evening, and to read their Greek Testament and to go to the pantomime. The Professor never tired of giving his students advice about the preservation of their bodily health. He strongly recommended a cold bath at six o'clock every morning. In winter, he remarked genially, you can break the ice with a hammer. According to himself, only one enthusiast seems to have followed his advice, and he died.

In Blackie's classroom there used to be a demonstration every time he mentioned the name of a distinguished politician. Whether the demonstration took the Professor by surprise, or whether he waited for it, will never, perhaps, be known. But Blackie at least put out the gleam in his eye, and looked as if he were angry. " I will say Beaconsfield," he would exclaim (cheers and hisses). " Beaconsfield " (uproar). Then he would stride forward, and, seizing the railing, announce his intention of saying Beaconsfield until every goose in the room was tired of cackling.

("Question.") "Beaconsfield." ("No no.")
"Beaconsfield." ("Hear, hear," and shouts
of "Gladstone.") "Beaconsfield." ("Three
cheers for Dizzy.") Eventually the class
would be dismissed as—(1) idiots, (2) a bear
garden, (3) a flock of sheep, (4) a pack of
numskulls, (5) hissing serpents. The professor would retire, apparently fuming, to his
anteroom, and five minutes afterwards he
would be playing himself down the North
Bridge on imaginary bagpipes. This sort of
thing added a sauce to all academic sessions.
There was a notebook also, which appeared
year after year. It contained the Professor's
jokes of a former session, carefully classified
by an admiring student. It was handed
down from one year's men to the next, and
thus if Blackie began to make a joke about
haggis, the possessor of the book had only
swiftly to turn to the H's, find what the joke
was, and send it along the class quicker than
the professor could speak it.

In the old days the Greek professor recited
a poem in honour of the end of the session.
He composed it himself, and, as known to me, it

took the form of a graduate's farewell to his
Alma Mater. Sometimes he would knock a
map down as if overcome with emotion, and
at critical moments a student in the back-
benches would accompany him on a penny
trumpet. Now, I believe, the Hellenic Club
takes the place of the classroom. All the
eminent persons in Edinburgh attends its
meetings, and Blackie, the Athenian, is in
the chair. The policeman in Douglas
Crescent looks skeered when you ask him
what takes place on these occasions. It is
generally understood that toward the end
of the meeting they agree to read Greek next
time.

IV.

PROFESSOR CALDERWOOD.

HERE is a true story that the general reader may jump, as it is intended for Professor Calderwood himself. Some years ago an English daily paper reviewed a book entitled "A Handbook of Moral Philosophy." The Professor knows the work. The "notice" was done by the junior reporter, to whom philosophical treatises are generally entrusted. He dealt leniently, on the whole, with Professor Calderwood, even giving him a word of encouragement here and there. Still the criticism was severe. The reviewer subsequently went to Edinburgh University, and came out 144th in the class of Moral Philosophy.

That student is now, I believe, on friendly terms with Professor Calderwood, but has never told him this story. I fancy the Professor would like to know his name. It may, perhaps, be reached in this way. He was the young gentleman who went to his classes the first day in a black coat and silk hat, and was cheered round the quadrangle by a body of admiring fellow-students, who took him for a professor.

Calderwood contrives to get himself more in touch with the mass of his students than some of his fellow-professors, partly because he puts a high ideal before himself, and to some extent because his subject is one that Scottish students revel in. Long before they join his class they know that they are moral philosophers; indeed, they are sometimes surer of it before they enrol than afterwards. Their essays begin in some such fashion as this—"In joining issue with Reid, I wish to take no unfair advantage of my antagonist"; or "Kant is sadly at fault when he says that"; or "It is strange that a man of Locke's attainments should have been blind to the fact." When the Professor reads out these tit-bits to the class his eyes twinkle. Some students, of course, are not such keen philosophers as others. Does Professor

Calderwood remember the one who was never struck by anything in moral philosophy until he learned by accident that Descartes lay in bed till about twelve o'clock every morning? Then it dawned on him that he, too, must have been a philosopher all his life without knowing it. One year a father and son were in the class. The father got so excited over volition and the line that divides right from wrong, that he wrenched the desk before him from its sockets and hit it triumphantly, meaning that he and the Professor were at one. He was generally admired by his fellow-students, because he was the only one in the class who could cry out " Hear, hear," and even " question," without blushing. The son, on the other hand, was *blasé*, and would have been an agnostic, only he could never remember the name. Once a week Calderwood turns his class into a debating society, and argues things out with his students. This field-day is a joy to them. Some of them spend the six days previous in preparing posers. The worst of the Professor is that he never sees that they are posers. What is the use of getting up a question of the most subtle kind, when he answers it right away? It makes you sit down quite suddenly. There is an occasional student who tries to convert liberty of speech on the discussion day into license, and of him the Professor makes short work. The student means to turn the laugh on Calderwood, and then Calderwood takes advantage of him, and the other students laugh at the wrong person. It is the older students, as a rule, who are most violently agitated over these philosophical debates. One with a beard cracks his fingers, after the manner of a child in a village school that knows who won the battle of Bannockburn, and feels that he must burst if he does not let it out at once. A bald-headed man rises every minute to put a question, and then sits down, looking stupid. He has been trying so hard to remember what it is, that he has forgotten. There is a legend of two who quarrelled over the Will and fought it out on Arthur's Seat.

One year, however, a boy of sixteen or so,

with a squeaky voice and a stammer, was
Calderwood's severest critic. He sat on the
back bench, and what he wanted to know
was something about the infinite. Every
discussion day he took advantage of a lull
in the debate to squeak out, "With regard to
the infinite," and then could never get any
further. No one ever discovered what he
wanted enlightenment on about the infinite.
He grew despondent as the session wore on,
but courageously stuck to his point. Probably he is a soured man now. For purposes
of exposition Calderwood has a black board
in his lecture-room, on which he chalks circles
that represent the feelings and the will, with
arrows shooting between them. In my class
there was a boy, a very little boy, who had
been a dux at school and was a dunce at
college. He could not make moral philosophy out at all, but did his best. Here were
his complete notes for one day :—" Edinburgh
University, class of Moral Philosophy, Professor Calderwood, Lecture 64, Jan. 11, 18—.
You rub out the arrow, and there is only the
circle left."

Professor Calderwood is passionately fond of music, as those who visit at his house know. He is of opinion that there is a great deal of moral philosophy in "The Dead March in Saul." Once he said something to that effect in his class, adding enthusiastically that he could excuse the absence of a student who had been away hearing "The Dead March in Saul." After that he received a good many letters from students, worded in this way : " Mr. McNaughton (bench 7) presents his compliments to Professor Calderwood, and begs to state that his absence from the class yesterday was owing to his being elsewhere, hearing 'The Dead March in Saul.'" " Dear Professor Calderwood — I regret my absence from the lecture to-day, but hope you will overlook it, as I was unavoidably detained at home, practising ' The Dead March in Saul.'—Yours truly, PETER WEBSTER." " Professor Calderwood,—Dear Sir,—As I was coming to the lecture to-day, I heard ' The Dead March in Saul ' being played in the street. You will, I am sure, make allowance for my non-attendance at the class, as I was too much affected to come. It is indeed a grand march.—Yours faithfully, JOHN ROBBIE." " The students whose names are subjoined thank the Professor of Moral Philosophy most cordially for his remarks on the elevating power of music. They have been encouraged thereby to start a class for the proper study of the impressive and solemn march to which he called special attention, and hope he will excuse them, should their practisings occasionally prevent their attendance at the Friday lectures." Professor Calderwood does not lecture on " The Dead March in Saul " now.

The class of Moral Philosophy is not for the few, but the many. Some professors do not mind what becomes of the nine students, so long as they can force on every tenth. Calderwood, however, considers it his duty to carry the whole class along with him, and it is, as a consequence, almost impossible to fall behind. The lectures are not delivered, in the ordinary sense, but dictated. Having explained the subject of the day with the

lucidity that is this professor's peculiar gift,
he condenses his remarks into a proposition.
It is as if a minister ended his sermon with
the text.   Thus :—" Proposition 34.   Man is
born into the world—(You have got that ?
See that you have all got it.)   Man is born
into the world with a capacity—with a
capacity—"   (Anxious student : " If you
please, Professor, where did you say man was
born into ?")   " Into the world, with a
capacity to distinguish "—(" With a what,
sir ?")—" with a capacity to distinguish "—
(Student : " Who is born into the world ? ")
" Perhaps I have been reading too quickly.
Man is born into the world, with a capacity
to distinguish between—distinguish between
(student shuts his book, thinking that com-
pletes the proposition)—distinguish between
right and wrong—right—and wrong.   You
have all got Proposition 34, gentlemen ? "

Once Calderwood was questioning a student
about a proposition to see that he thoroughly
understood it.   " Give an illustration," suggested the Professor.   The student took the
case of a murderer.   " Very good," said the

Professor. "Now give me another illustration." The student pondered for a little. "Well," he said at length, "take the case of another murderer."

Professor Calderwood has such an exceptional interest in his students that he asks every one of them to his house. This is but one of many things that makes him generally popular ; he also invites his ladies' class to meet them. The lady whom you take down to supper suggests Proposition 41 as a nice thing to talk about, and asks what you think of the metaphysics of ethics. Professor Calderwood sees the ladies into the cabs himself. It is the only thing I ever heard against him.

V.

PROFESSOR TAIT.

JUST as I opened my desk to write enthusiastically of Tait, I remembered having
recently deciphered a pencil note about him,
in my own handwriting, on the cover of
Masson's "Chronological List," which I still
keep by me. I turned to the note to see if
there was life in it yet. "Walls," it says,
"got 2s. for T. and T. at Brown's, 16, Walker-
street." I don't recall Walls, but T. and T.
was short for "Thomson and Tait's Elements
of Natural Philosophy" (Elements !), better
known in my year as the "Student's First
Glimpse of Hades." Evidently Walls sold
his copy, but why did I take such note of the
address? I fear T. and T. is one of the
Books Which Have Helped Me. This some-
what damps my ardour.

When Tait was at Cambridge it was flung

in the face of the mathematicians that they never stood high in Scriptural knowledge. Tait and another were the two of whom one must be first wrangler, and they agreed privately to wipe this stigma from mathematics. They did it by taking year about the prize which was said to hang out of their reach. It is always interesting to know of professors who have done well in Biblical knowledge. All Scottish students at the English Universities are not so successful. I knew a Snell man who was sent back from the Oxford entrance exam., and he always held himself that the Biblical questions had done it.

Turner is said by medicals to be the finest lecturer in the University. He will never be that so long as Tait is in the Natural Philosophy chair. Never, I think, can there have been a more superb demonstrator. I have his burly figure before me. The small twinkling eyes had a fascinating gleam in them; he could concentrate them until they held the object looked at; when they flashed round the room he seemed to have drawn a rapier. I have seen a man fall back in alarm under Tait's eyes, though there were a dozen benches between them. These eyes could be merry as a boy's, though, as when he turned a tube of water on students who would insist on crowding too near an experiment, for Tait's was the humour of high spirits. I could conceive him at marbles still, and feeling annoyed at defeat. He could not fancy anything much funnier than a man missing his chair. Outside his own subject he is not, one feels, a six-footer. When Mr. R. L. Stevenson's memoir of the late Mr. Fleeming Jenkin was published, Tait said at great length that he did not like it; he would have had the sketch by a scientific man. But though scientists may be the only men nowadays who have anything to say, they are also the only men who can't say it. Scientific men out of their sphere know for a fact that novels are not true. So they draw back from novelists who write biography, Professor Tait and Mr. Stevenson are both men of note, who walk different ways, and when they meet neither likes to take the curbstone.

If they were tied together for life in a three-legged race, which would suffer the more?

But if Tait's science weighs him to the earth, he has a genius for sticking to his subject, and I am lost in admiration every time I bring back his lectures. It comes as natural to his old students to say when they meet, "What a lecturer Tait was!" as to Englishmen to joke about the bagpipes. It is not possible to draw a perfect circle, Chrystal used to say, after drawing a very fine one. To the same extent it was not possible for Tait never to fail in his experiments. The atmosphere would be too much for him once in a session, or there were other hostile influences at work. Tait warned us of these before proceeding to experiment, but we merely smiled. We believed in him as though he were a Bradshaw announcing that he would not be held responsible for possible errors.

I had forgotten Lindsay; "the mother may forget her child." As I write he has slipped back into his chair on the Professor's right, and I could photograph him now in his brown suit. Lindsay was the imperturbable man who assisted Tait in his experiments, and his father held the post before him. When there were many of us together, we could applaud Lindsay with burlesque exaggeration, and he treated us good-humouredly, as making something considerable between us. But I once had to face Lindsay alone, in quest of my certificate; and suddenly he towered above me, as a waiter may grow tall when you find that you have not money enough to pay the bill. He treated me most kindly; did not reply, of course, but got the certificate, and handed it to me as a cashier contemptuously shovels you your pile of gold. Long ago I pasted up a crack in my window with the certificate, but it said, I remember, that I had behaved respectably—so far as I had come under the eyes of the Professor. Tait was always an enthusiast.

We have been keeping Lindsay waiting. When he had nothing special to do he sat indifferently in his chair, with the face of a precentor after the sermon has begun. But though it was not very likely that Lindsay

would pay much attention to talk about such
playthings as the laws of Nature, his fingers
went out in the direction of the Professor
when the experiments began. Then he was
not the precentor; he was a minister in one
of the pews. Lindsay was an inscrutable
man, and I shall not dare to say that he even
half-wished to see Tait fail. He only looked
on, ready for any emergency; but if the
experiment would not come off, he was as
quick to go to the Professor's assistance as
a member of Parliament is to begin when
he has caught the Speaker's eye. Perhaps
Tait would have none of his aid, or pushed
the mechanism for the experiment from him
— an intimation to Lindsay to carry it
quickly to the ante-room. Do you think
Lindsay read the instructions so? Let me
tell you that your mind fails to seize hold
of Lindsay. He marched the machine out
of Tait's vicinity as a mother may push her
erring boy away from his father's arms, to
take him to her heart as soon as the door
is closed. Lindsay took the machine to his
seat, and laid it before him on the desk with

well-concealed apathy. Tait would flash his
eye to the right to see what Lindsay was
after, and there was Lindsay sitting with his
arms folded. The Professor's lecture resumed
its way, and then out went Lindsay's hands
to the machine. Here he tried a wheel ;
again he turned a screw ; in time he had
the machine ready for another trial. No
one was looking his way, when suddenly
there was a whizz — bang, bang. All eyes
were turned upon Lindsay, the Professor's
among them. A cheer broke out as we
realized that Lindsay had done the experiment. Was he flushed with triumph ? Not
a bit of it ; he was again sitting with his
arms folded. A Glasgow merchant of modest
manners, when cross-examined in a law court,
stated that he had a considerable monetary
interest in a certain concern. " How much
do you mean by a 'considerable monetary
interest' ? " demanded the contemptuous bar-
rister who was cross-examining him. " Oh,"
said the witness, humbly, " a maiter o' a
million an' a half — or, say, twa million."
That Glasgow man in the witness-box is the

only person I can think of when looking about me for a parallel to Lindsay. While the Professor eyed him and the students deliriously beat the floor, Lindsay quietly gathered the mechanism together and carried it to the ante-room. His head was not flung back nor his chest forward, like one who walked to music. In his hour of triumph he was still imperturbable. I lie back in my chair to-day, after the lapse of years, and ask myself again, How did Lindsay behave after he entered the ante-room, shutting the door behind him? Did he give way? There is no one to say. When he returned to the classroom he wore his familiar face; a man to ponder over.

There is a legend about the Natural Philo-sophy classroom—the period long antecedent to Tait. The Professor, annoyed by a habit students had got into of leaving their hats on his desk, announced that the next hat placed there would be cut in pieces by him in pre-sence of the class. The warning had its effect, until one day when the Professor was called for a few minutes from the room. An undergraduate, to whom the natural sciences, unrelieved, were a monotonous study, slipped into the ante-room, from which he emerged with the Professor's hat. This he placed on the desk, and then stole in a panic to his seat. An awe fell upon the class. The Professor returned, but when he saw the hat he stopped. He showed no anger. "Gentlemen," he said, "I told you what would happen if you again disobeyed my orders." Quite blandly he took a pen-knife from his pocket, slit the hat into several pieces, and flung them into the sink. While the hat was under the knife the students forgot to demonstrate, but as it splashed into the sink they gave forth a true British cheer. The end.

Close to the door of the Natural Philosophy room is a window that in my memory will ever be sacred to a janitor. The janitors of the University were of varied interest, from the merry one who treated us as if we were his equals, and the soldier who sometimes looked as if he would like to mow us down, to the Head Man of All, whose name I dare not write, though I can

whisper it. The janitor at the window, however, sat there through the long evenings
while the Debating Society (of which I was
a member) looked after affairs of State in
an adjoining room. We were the smallest
society in the University and the longest-
winded, and I was once nearly expelled for
not paying my subscription. Our grand
debate was, " Is the policy of the Government worthy the confidence of this Society?"
and we also read about six essays yearly
on "The Genius of Robert Burns"; but it
was on private business that we came out
strongest. The question that agitated us
most was whether the meetings should be
opened with prayer, and the men who
thought they should would not so much as
look at the men who thought they should not.
When the janitor was told that we had begun
our private business he returned to his window and slept. His great day was when we
could not form a quorum, which happened
now and then.

Gregory was a member of that society:
what has become of Gregory? He was one of

those men who professors say have a brilliant future before them, and who have not since been heard of. Morton, another member, was of a different stamp. He led in the debate on " Beauty of the Mind v. Beauty of the Body." His writhing contempt for the beauty that is only skin deep is not to be forgotten. How noble were his rhapsodies on the beauty of the mind! And when he went to Calderwood's to supper, how quick he was to pick out the prettiest girl, who took ten per cent. in Moral Philosophy, and to sit beside her all the evening. Morton had a way of calling on his friends the night before a degree examination to ask them to put him up to as much as would pull him through.

Tait used to get greatly excited over the rectorial elections, and if he could have disguised himself, would have liked, I think, to join in the fight round the Brewster statue. He would have bled for the Conservative cause, as his utterances on University reform have shown. The reformers have some cause for thinking that Tait is a greater man in his classroom than when he addresses the graduates. He has said that the less his students know of his subject when they join his class, the less, probably, they will have to unlearn. Such views are behind the times that feed their children on geographical biscuits in educational nurseries with astronomical ceilings and historical wall-papers.

VI.

PROFESSOR CAMPBELL FRASER.

NOT long ago I was back in the Old University — how well I remember pointing it out as the gaol to a stranger who had asked me to show him round. I was in one of the library ante-rooms, when some one knocked, and I looked up, to see Campbell Fraser framed in the doorway. I had not looked on that venerable figure for half a dozen years. I had forgotten all my metaphysics. Yet it all came back with a rush. I was on my feet, wondering if I existed strictly so-called.

Calderwood and Fraser had both their followings. The moral philosophers wore an air of certainty, for they knew that if they stuck to Calderwood he would pull them through. You cannot lose yourself in the back-garden. But the metaphysicians had their doubts. Fraser led them into strange

places, and said he would meet them there
again next day. They wandered to their
lodgings, and got into difficulties with their
landlady for saying that she was only an
aggregate of sense phenomena. Fraser was
rather a hazardous cure for weak intellects.
Young men whose anchor had been certainty
of themselves went into that class floating
buoyantly on the sea of facts, and came out
all adrift—on the sea of theory—in an open
boat—rudderless—one oar—the boat scuttled.
How could they think there was any chance
for them, when the Professor was not even
sure of himself? I see him rising in a daze
from his chair and putting his hands through
his hair. " Do I exist," he said, thoughtfully,
" strictly so-called ? " The students (if it was
the beginning of the session) looked a little
startled. This was a matter that had not
previously disturbed them. Still, if the Professor was in doubt, there must be something
in it. He began to argue it out, and an
uncomfortable silence held the room in awe.
If he did not exist, the chances were that they
did not exist either. It was thus a personal

question. The Professor glanced round slowly
for an illustration. "Am I a table?" A
pained look travelled over the class. Was it
just possible that they were all tables? It is
no wonder that the students who do not go to
the bottom during their first month of metaphysics begin to give themselves airs strictly
so-called. In the privacy of their room at
the top of the house they pinch themselves to
see if they are still there.

He would, I think, be a sorry creature who
did not find something to admire in Campbell
Fraser. Metaphysics may not trouble you, as
it troubles him, but you do not sit under the
man without seeing his transparent honesty
and feeling that he is genuine. In appearance and in habit of thought he is an ideal
philosopher, and his communings with himself
have lifted him to a level of serenity that is
worth struggling for. Of all the arts professors in Edinburgh he is probably the most
difficult to understand, and students in a hurry
have called his lectures childish. If so, it may
be all the better for them. For the first half
of the hour, they say, he tells you what he is

going to do, and for the second half he revises. Certainly he is vastly explanatory, but then he is not so young as they are, and so he has his doubts. They are so cock-sure that they wonder to see him hesitate. Often there is a mist on the mountain when it is all clear in the valley.

Fraser's great work in his edition of Berkeley, a labour of love that should live after him. He has two Berkeleys, the large one and the little one, and, to do him justice, it was the little one he advised us to consult. I never read the large one myself, which is in a number of monster tomes, but I often had a look at it in the library, and I was proud to think that an Edinburgh professor was the editor. When Glasgow men came through to talk of their professors we showed them the big Berkeley, and after that they were reasonable. There was one man in my year who really began the large Berkeley, but after a time he was missing, and it is believed that some day he will be found flattened between the pages of the first volume.

The " Selections " was the text-book we

used in the class.   It is sufficient to prove that
Berkeley wrote beautiful English.   I am not
sure that any one has written such English
since.   We have our own " stylists," but how
self-conscious they are after Berkeley.   It is
seven years since I opened my " Selections,"
but I see that I was once more of a metaphysician than I have been giving myself credit
for.   The book is scribbled over with posers in
my handwriting about dualism and primary
realities.   Some of the comments are in short-
hand, which I must at one time have been
able to read, but all are equally unintelligible
now.   Here is one of my puzzlers :—" Does
B here mean impercipient and unperceived
subject or conscious and percipient subject ? "
Observe the friendly B.   I daresay farther on
I shall find myself referring to the Professor
as F.   I wonder if I ever discovered what B
meant.   I could not now tell what I meant
myself.

   As many persons are aware, the " Selections "
consist of Berkeley's text with the Professor's notes thereon.   The notes are explanatory of the text, and the student must find

them an immense help. Here, for instance,
is a note :—" Phenomenal or sense dependent
existence can be substantiated and caused
only by a self-conscious spirit, for otherwise
there could be no propositions about it expres-
sive of what is conceivable ; on the other
hand, to affirm that phenomenal or sense
dependent existence, which alone we know,
and which alone is conceivable, is, or even
represents, an inconceivable non-phenomenal
or abstract existence, would be to affirm a
contradiction in terms." There we have it.

As a metaphysician I was something of a
disappointment. I began well, standing, if I
recollect aright, in the three examinations,
first, seventeenth, and seventy-seventh. A
man who sat beside me—man was the word
we used—gazed at me reverently when I
came out first, and I could see by his eye
that he was not sure whether I existed
properly so-called. By the second exam. his
doubts had gone, and by the third he was
surer of me than of himself. He came out
fifty-seventh, this being the grand triumph of
his college course. He was the same whose

key translated *cras donaberis haedo* "To-morrow you will be presented with a kid," but who, thinking that a little vulgar, refined it down to "To-morrow you will be presented with a small child."

In the metaphysics class I was like the fountains in the quadrangle, which ran dry toward the middle of the session. While things were still looking hopeful for me, I had an invitation to breakfast with the Professor. If the fates had been so propitious as to forward me that invitation, it is possible that I might be a metaphysician to this day, but I had changed my lodgings, and when I heard of the affair, all was over. The Professor asked me to stay behind one day after the lecture, and told me that he had got his note back with " Left : no address," on it. "However," he said, "you may keep this," presenting me with the invitation for the Saturday previously. I mention this to show that even professors have hearts. That letter is preserved with the autographs of three editors, none of which anybody can read.

There was once a medical student who

came up to my rooms early in the session,
and I proved to him in half an hour that he
did not exist. He got quite frightened, and I
can still see his white face as he sat staring at
me in the gloaming. This shows what metaphysics can do. He has recovered, however,
and is sheep-farming now, his examiners never
having asked him the right questions.

The last time Fraser ever addressed me
was when I was capped. He said, "I congratulate you, Mr. Smith": and one of the
other professors said, "I congratulate you,
Mr. Fisher." My name is neither Smith nor
Fisher, but no doubt the thing was kindly
meant. It was then, however, that the professor of metaphysics had his revenge on me.
I had once spelt Fraser with a "z"

VII.

PROFESSOR CHRYSTAL.

WHEN Chrystal came to Edinburgh he rooted up the humours of the classroom as a dentist draws teeth. Souls were sold for keys that could be carried in the waistcoat pocket. Ambition fell from heights, and lay with its eye on a certificate. By night was a rush of ghosts, shrieking for passes. Horse play fled before the Differential Calculus in spectacles.

I had Chrystal's first year, and recall the gloomy student sitting before me who hacked "All hope abandon ye who enter here" into a desk that may have confined Carlyle. It took him a session, and he was digging his own grave, for he never got through; but it was something to hold by, something he felt sure of. All else was spiders' webs in chalk.

Chrystal was a fine hare for the hounds who could keep up with him. He started off the

first day with such a spurt that most of us
were left behind mopping our faces, and saying, "Here's a fellow," which is what Mr.
Stevenson says Shakespeare would have remarked about Mr. George Meredith. We
never saw him again. The men who were
on speaking acquaintance with his symbols
revelled in him as students love an enthusiast
who is eager to lead them into a world toward
which they would journey. He was a rare
guide for them. The bulk, however, lost him
in labyrinths. They could not but admire
their brilliant professor ; but while their friend
the medalist and he kept the conversation
to themselves, they felt like eavesdroppers
hearkening to a pair of lovers. " It is beautiful," they cried, " but this is no place for us ;
let us away."

A good many went, but their truancy stuck
in their throats like Otway's last roll. The
M.A. was before them. They had fancied it
in their hands, but it became shy as a maiden
from the day they learned Chrystal's heresy
that Euclid is not mathematics but only some
riders in it. This snapped the cord that had

tied the blind man to his dog, and the M.A. shot down the horizon. When Rutherford delivered his first lecture in the chair of Institutes of Medicine, boisterous students drowned his voice, and he flung out of the room. At the door he paused to say, "Gentlemen, we shall meet again at Philippi." A dire bomb was this in the midst of them, warranted to go off, none able to cast it overboard. We, too, had our Philippi before us. Chrystal could not be left to his own devices.

I had never a passion for knowing that when circles or triangles attempt impossibilities it is absurd ; and x was an unknown quantity I was ever content to walk round about. To admit to Chrystal that we understood x was only a way he had of leading you on to y and z. I gave him his chance, however, by contributing a paper of answers to his first weekly set of exercises. When the hour for returning the slips came round, I was there to accept fame—if so it was to be—with modesty ; and if it was to be humiliation, still to smile. The Professor said there was one paper, with an owner's name on it, which he could not read, and it was handed along the class to be deciphered. My presentiment that it was mine became a certainty when it reached my hand ; but I passed it on pleasantly, and it returned to Chrystal, a Japhet that never found its father. Feeling that the powers were against me, I then retired from the conflict, sanguine that the teaching of my mathematical schoolmaster, the best that could be, would pull me through. The Disowned may be going the round of the classroom still.

The men who did not know when they were beaten returned to their seats, and doggedly took notes, their faces lengthening daily. Their note-books reproduced exactly the hieroglyphics of the blackboard, and, examined at night, were as suggestive as the photographs of persons one has never seen. To overtake Chrystal after giving him a start was the presumption that is an offshoot from despair. There was once an elderly gentleman who for years read the *Times* every day from the first page to the last. For a fortnight he was ill of a fever ; but, on recovering, he began at the copy of the *Times* where he had left off. He struggled magnificently to make up on the *Times*, but it was in vain. This is an allegory for the way these students panted after Chrystal.

Some succumbed and joined the majority—literally ; for to mathematics they were dead. I never hear of the old University now, nor pass under the shadow of the walls one loves when he is done with them, without seeing myself as I was the day I matriculated, an awestruck boy, passing and repassing the gates, frightened to venture inside, breathing heavily at sight of janitors, Scott and Carlyle in the air. After that I see nothing fuller of colour than the meetings that were held outside Chrystal's door. Adjoining it is a class-room so little sought for, that legend tells of its door once showing the notice : " There will be no class to-day as the student is unwell." The crowd round Chrystal's could have filled that room. It was composed of students hearkening at the door to see whether he was to call their part of the roll to-day. If he did, they slunk in ; if not, the

crowd melted into the streets, this refrain in
their ears —

"I'm plucked, I do admit,
　I'm spun, my mother dear,
Yet do not grieve for that
　Which happens every year.
I've waited very patiently,
　I may have long to wait,
But you've another son, mother,
　And he will graduate."

A professor of mathematics once brought
a rowdy student from the back benches to a
seat beside him, because—"First, you'll be near
the board ; second, you'll be near me ; and,
third, you'll be near the door." Chrystal soon
discovered that students could be too near the
door, and he took to calling the roll in the
middle of the hour, which insured an increased
attendance. It was a silent class, nothing
heard but the patter of pencils, rats scraping
for grain, of which there was abundance, but
not one digestion in a bench. To smuggle
in a novel up one's waistcoat was perilous,
Chrystal's spectacles doing their work. At
a corner of the platform sat the assistant,
with a constable's authority, but not formed

for swooping, uneasy because he had legs, and where to put them he knew not. He got through the hour by shifting his position every five minutes; and, sitting there waiting, he reminded one of the boy who, on being told to remain so quietly where he was that he could hear a pin drop, held his breath a moment, then shouted, " Let it drop!" An excellent fellow was this assistant, who told us that one of his predecessors had got three months.

A jest went as far in that class as a plum in the midshipmen's pudding, and, you remember, when the middies came on a plum they gave three cheers. In the middle of some brilliant reasoning Chrystal would stop to add 4, 7, and 11. Addition of this kind was the only thing he could not do, and he looked to the class for help—" 20," they shouted, " 24," " 17," while he thought it over. These appeals to their intelligence made them beam. They woke up as a sleepy congregation shakes itself into life when the minister says, " I remember when I was a little boy. . . ."

The daring spirits—say, those who were

going into their father's office, and so did not
look upon Chrystal as a door locked to their
advancement—sought to bring sunshine into
the room. Chrystal soon had the blind down
on that. I hear they have been at it recently
with the usual result. To relieve the mono-
tony, a student at the end of bench ten dropped
a marble, which toppled slowly downward
toward the Professor. At every step it took
there was a smothered guffaw; but Chrystal,
who was working at the board, did not turn
his head. When the marble reached the
floor, he said, still with his back to the class,
" Will the student at the end of bench ten,
who dropped that marble, stand up?" All
eyes dilated. He had counted the falls of the
marble from step to step. Mathematics do
not obscure the intellect.

Twenty per cent. was a good percentage in
Chrystal's examinations; thirty sent you away
whistling. As the M.A. drew nigh, students
on their prospects might have been farmers
discussing the weather. Some put their faith
in the Professor's goodness of heart, of which
symptoms had been showing. He would

not, all at once, " raise the standard "—hated
phrase until you are through, when you write
to the papers advocating it. Courage ! was it
not told of the Glasgow Snell competition
that one of the competitors, as soon as he saw
the first paper, looked for his hat and the door,
that he was forbidden to withdraw until an
hour had elapsed, and that he then tackled
the paper and ultimately carried off the Snell ?
Of more immediate interest, perhaps, was the
story of the quaking student, whose neighbour
handed him in pencil, beneath the desk, the
answer to several questions. It was in an
M.A. exam., and the affrighted student found
that he could not read his neighbour's notes.
Trusting to fortune, he enclosed them with his
own answers, writing at the top, " No time to
write these out in ink, so enclose them in
pencil." He got through : no moral.

A condemned criminal wondering if he is
to get a reprieve will not feel the position
novel, if he has loitered in a University quadrangle waiting for the janitor to nail up the
results of a degree exam. A queer gathering
we were, awaiting the verdict of Chrystal.

Some compressed their lips, others were lively
as fireworks dipped in water ; there were those
who rushed round and round the quadrangle ;
only one went the length of saying that he
did not want to pass. H. I shall call him. I
met him the other day in Fleet Street, and he
annoyed me by asking at once if I remembered the landlady I quarrelled with because
she wore my socks to church of a Sunday :
we found her out one wet forenoon. H.
waited the issue with a cigar in his mouth.
He had purposely, he explained, given in a
bad paper. He could not understand why
men were so anxious to get through. He had
ten reasons for wishing to be plucked. We
let him talk. The janitor appeared with the
fateful paper, and we lashed about him like
waves round a lighthouse, all but H., who
strolled languidly to the board to which the
paper was being fastened. A moment afterwards I heard a shriek, " I'm through ! I'm
through ! " It was H. His cigar was dashed
aside, and he sped like an arrow from the bow
to the nearest telegraph office, shouting " I'm
through ! " as he ran.

Those of us who had H.'s fortune now consider Chrystal made to order for his chair, but he has never, perhaps, had a proper appreciation of the charming fellows who get ten per cent.

VIII.

WHEN one of the distinguished hunting
ladies who chase celebrities captured
Mr. Mark Pattison, he gave anxious con-
sideration to the quotation which he was
asked to write above his name. " Fancy,"
he said with a shudder, "going down to
posterity arm in arm with *carpe diem!* "
Remembering this, I forbear tying Sellar to
odi profanum vulgus. Yet the name opens
the door to the quotation.

Sellar is a Roman senator. He stood
very high at Oxford, and took a prize for
boxing. If you watch him in the class, you
will sometimes see his mind murmuring that
Edinburgh students do not take their play
like Oxford men. The difference is in manner. A courteous fellow-student of Sellar
once showed his relatives over Balliol. " You
have now, I think," he said at last, "seen

everything of interest except the Master." He flung a stone at a window, at which the Master's head appeared immediately, menacing, wrathful. "And now," concluded the polite youth, "you have seen him also."

Mr. James Payn, who never forgave the Scottish people for pulling down their blinds on Sundays, was annoyed by the halo they have woven around the name "Professor." He knew an Edinburgh lady who was scandalized because that mere poet, Alexander Smith, coolly addressed professors by their surnames. Mr. Payn might have known what it is to walk in the shadow of a Senatus Academicus, could he have met such specimens as Sellar, Fraser, Tait, and Sir Alexander Grant marching down the Bridges abreast. I have seen them : an inspiriting sight. The pavement only held three. You could have shaken hands with them from an upper window.

Sellar's treatment of his students was always that of a fine gentleman. Few got near him ; all respected him. At times he was addressed in an unknown tongue, but he

kept his countenance. He was particular
about students keeping to their proper
benches, and once thought he had caught
a swarthy north countryman straying. " You
are in your wrong seat, Mr. Orr." " Na, am
richt eneuch." " You should be in the seat
in front. That is bench 12, and you are
entered on bench 10." " Eh? This is no
bench twal, (counting) twa, fower, sax, aucht,
ten." "There is something wrong." " Oh-h-h
(with sudden enlightenment) ye've been coun-
tin' the first dask ; we dinna coont the first
dask." The Professor knew the men he had
to deal with too well to scorn this one, who
turned out to be a fine fellow. He was the
only man I ever knew who ran his medical
and arts classes together, and so many lectures
had he to attend daily that he mixed them up.
He graduated, however, in both faculties in
five years, and the last I heard of him was
that, when applying for a medical assistant-
ship, he sent his father's photograph because
he did not have one of himself. He was a
man of brains as well as sinew, and dined
briskly on a shilling a week.

There was a little fellow in the class who was a puzzle to Sellar, because he was higher sitting than standing: when the Professor asked him to stand up, he stood down. "Is Mr. Blank not present?" Sellar would ask. "Here, sir," cried Blank. "Then, will you stand up, Mr. Blank?" (Agony of Blank, and a demonstration of many feet.) "Are you not prepared, Mr. Blank?" "Yes, sir; *Pastor quum traharet—*" "I insist on your standing up, Mr. Blank." (Several students rise to their feet to explain, but subside.) "Yes, sir; *Pastor quum traharet per—*" "I shall mark you 'not prepared,' Mr. Blank." (Further demonstration, and then an indignant squeak from Blank.) "If you please, sir, I am standing." "But, in that case, how is it—? Ah, oh, ah, yes; proceed, Mr. Blank." As one man was only called upon for exhibition five or six times in a year, the Professor had always forgotten the circumstances when he asked Blank to stand up again. Blank was looked upon by his fellow-students as a practical jest, and his name was always received with the prolonged applause which greets the end of an after-dinner speech.

Sellar never showed resentment to the students who addressed him as Professor Sellars.

One day the Professor was giving out some English to be translated into Latin prose. He read on—" and fiercely lifting the axe with both hands—" when a cheer from the top bench made him pause. The cheer spread over the room like an uncorked gas. Sellar frowned, but proceeded—" lifting the axe—," when again the class became demented. " What does this mean ? " he demanded, looking as if he, too, could lift the axe. " Axe ! " shouted a student in explanation. Still Sellar could not solve the riddle. Another student rose to his assistance. " Axe—Gladstone ! " he cried. Sellar sat back in his chair. " Really, gentlemen," he said, " I take the most elaborate precautions against touching upon politics in this class, but sometimes you are beyond me. Let us continue—' and fiercely lifting his weapon with both hands—.' "

The duxes from the schools suffered a little during their first year, from a feeling that they and Sellar understood each other. He liked to undeceive them. We had one, all head, who went about wondering at himself. He lost his bursary on the way home with it, and still he strutted. Sellar asked if we saw anything peculiar in a certain line from Horace. We did not. We were accustomed to trust to Horace's reputation, all but the dandy. "Eh—ah! Professor," he lisped; "it ought to have been so and so." Sellar looked at this promising plant from the schools, and watered him without a rose on the pan. "Depend upon it, Mr.—; ah, I did not catch your name, if it ought to have been so and so, Horace would have made it so and so."

Sellar's face was proof against sudden wit. It did not relax till he gave it liberty. You could never tell from it what was going on inside. He read without a twitch a notice on his door : " Found in this class a gold-headed pencil case ; if not claimed within three days will be sold to defray expenses." He even withstood the battering ram on the day of the publication of his " Augustan Poets." The students could not let this opportunity pass. They assailed him with frantic applause every bench was a drum to thump upon. His countenance said nothing. The drums had it in the end, though, and he dismissed the class with what is believed to have verged on a smile. Like the lover who has got his lady's glance, they at once tried for more, but no.

Most of us had Humanity our first year, which is the year for experimenting. Then is the time to join the University library. The pound, which makes you a member, has never had its poet. You can withdraw your pound when you please. There are far-seeing men who work the whole thing out by mathematics. Put simply, this is the notion. In the beginning of the session you join the library, and soon you forget about your pound ; you reckon without it. As the winter closes in, and the coal-bunk empties ; or you find that five shillings a week for lodgings is a dream that cannot be kept up ; or your coat assumes more and more the colour identified with spring; or you would feast your friends for once right gloriously; or next Wednesday is your little sister's birthday; you cower, despairing, over a sulky fire. Suddenly you are on your feet, all aglow once more. What is this thought that sends the blood to your head? That library pound! You had forgotten that you had a bank. Next morning you are at the university in time to help the library door to open. You ask for your pound; you get it. Your hand mounts guard over the pocket in which it rustles. So they say. I took their advice and paid in my money; then waited exultingly to forget about it. In vain. I always allowed for that pound in my thoughts. I saw it as plainly, I knew its every feature as a schoolboy remembers his first trout. Not to be hasty, I gave my pound two months, and then brought it home again. I had a fellow-student who lived across the way from me. We railed at the library pound theory at open windows over the life of the street; a beautiful dream, but mad, mad.

He was an enthusiast, and therefore happy, whom I have seen in the Humanity class-room on an examination day, his pen racing with time, himself seated in the contents of an ink-bottle. Some stories of exams. have even a blacker ending. I write in tears of him who, estimating his memory as a leaky vessel, did with care and forethought draw up a crib that was more condensed than a pocket cyclopædia, a very Liebig's essence of the classics, tinned meat for students in the eleventh hour. Bridegrooms have been known to forget the ring; this student forgot his crib. In the middle of the examination came a nervous knocking at the door. A lady wanted to see the Professor at once. The student looked up, to see his mother handing the Professor his crib. Her son had forgotten it; she was sure that it was important, so she had brought it herself.

Jump the body of this poor victim. There was no M.A. for him that year; but in our gowns and sashes we could not mourn for a might-have-been. Soldiers talk of the Victoria Cross, statesmen of the Cabinet, ladies

of a pearl set in diamonds. These are pretty
baubles, but who has thrilled as the student
that with bumping heart strolls into Middle-
mass's to order his graduate's gown. He
hires it—five shillings—but the photograph
to follow makes it as good as his for life.
Look at him, young ladies, as he struts to
the Synod Hall to have M.A. tacked to his
name. Dogs do not dare bark at him. His
gait is springy ; in Princes Street he is as one
who walks upstairs. Gone to me are those
student days for ever, but I can still put a
photograph before me of a ghost in gown and
cape, the hair straggling under the cap as
tobacco may straggle over the side of a tin
when there is difficulty in squeezing down the
lid. How well the little black jacket looks,
how vividly the wearer remembers putting it
on. He should have worn a dress-coat, but
he had none. The little jacket resembled
one with the tails off, and, as he artfully
donned his gown, he backed against the wall
so that no one might know.

To turn up the light on old college days is
not always the signal for the dance. You are

back in the dusty little lodging, with its battered sofa, its slippery tablecloth, the prim array of books, the picture of the death of Nelson, the peeling walls, the broken clock; you are again in the quadrangle with him who has been dead this many a year. There are tragedies in a college course. Dr. Walter Smith has told in a poem mentioned elsewhere of the brilliant scholar who forgot his dominie; some, alas! forget their mother. There are men—I know it—who go mad from loneliness; and medalists ere now have crept home to die. The capping-day was the end of our spring-tide, and for some of us the summer was to be brief. Sir Alexander, gone into the night since then, flung " I mekemae " at us as we trooped past him, all in bud, some small flower to blossom in time, let us hope, here and there.

IX

MR. JOSEPH THOMSON.

TWO years hence Joseph Thomson's reputation will be a decade old, though he
is at present only thirty years of age. When
you meet him for the first time you con-
clude that he must be the explorer's son.
His identity, however, can always be proved
by simply mentioning Africa in his presence.
Then he draws himself up, and his eyes
glisten, and he is thinking how glorious it
would be to be in the Masai country again,
living on meat so diseased that it crumbled
in the hand like short-bread.

Gatelaw-bridge Quarry, in Dumfriesshire, is
famous for Old Mortality and Thomson, the
latter (when he is at the head of a caravan)
being as hardheaded as if he had been cut
out of it. He went to school at Thornhill,
where he spent great part of his time in
reading novels, and then he matriculated at

Edinburgh University, where he began to accumulate medals. Geology and kindred studies were his favourites there. One day he heard that Keith Johnston, then on the point of starting for Africa, wanted a lieutenant. Thomson was at that time equally in need of a Keith Johnston, and everybody who knew him saw that the opening and he were made for each other. Keith Johnston and Thomson went out together, and Johnston died in the jungle. This made a man in an hour of a stripling. Most youths in Thomson's position at that turning point of his career would have thought it judicious to turn back, and in geographical circles it would have been considered highly creditable had he brought his caravan to the coast intact. Thomson, however, pushed on, and did everything that his dead leader had hoped to do. From that time his career has been followed by every one interested in African exploration, and by his countrymen with some pride in addition. When an expedition was organized for the relief of Emin Pasha, there was for a time some probability of Thomson's having the command. He and Stanley differed as to the routes that should be taken, and subsequent events have proved that Thomson's was the proper one.

Thomson came over from Paris at that time to consult with the authorities, and took up his residence in the most over-grown hotel in London. His friends here organized an expedition for his relief. They wandered up and down the endless stairs looking for him, till, had they not wanted to make themselves a name, they would have beaten a retreat. He also wandered about looking for them, and at last they met. The leader of the party, restraining his emotion, lifted his hat, and said, "Mr. Thomson, I presume?" This is how I found Thomson.

The explorer had been for some months in Paris at that time, and France did him the honour of translating his "Through Masai-land" into French. In this book there is a picture of a buffalo tossing Thomson in the air. This was after he had put several bullets into it, and in the sketch he is represented some ten feet from the ground, with

his gun flying one way and his cap another.
" It was just as if I were distributing largess
to the natives," the traveller says now, though
this idea does not seem to have struck him
at the time. He showed the sketch to a
Parisian lady, who looked at it long and
earnestly. " Ah, M. Thomson," she said at
length, " but how could you pose like that ? "

Like a good many other travellers, inclu-
ding Mr. Du Chaillu, who says he is a dear
boy, Thomson does not smoke. Stanley,
however, smokes very strong cigars, as those
who have been in his sumptuous chambers in
Bond Street can testify. All the three happen to be bachelors, though ; because, one
of them says, after returning from years of
lonely travel, a man has such a delight in
female society that to pick and choose would
be invidious. Yet they have had their
chance. An African race once tried to bribe
Mr. Du Chaillu with a kingdom and over
eight hundred wives,—" the biggest offer," he
admits, " I ever had in one day."

Among the lesser annoyances to which
Thomson was subjected in Africa was the

presence of rats in the night-time, which he had to brush away like flies. Until he was asked whether there was not danger in this, it never seems to have struck him that it was more than annoying. Yet though he and the two other travellers mentioned (doubtless they are not alone in this) have put up cheerfully with almost every hardship known to man, this does not make them indifferent to the comforts of civilization when they return home. Du Chaillu was looking very comfortable in a house-boat the other day, where his hosts thought they were "roughing it"—with a male attendant ; and in Stanley's easy chairs you sink to dream. The last time I saw Thomson in his rooms in London he was on his knees, gazing in silent rapture at a china saucer with a valuable crack in it.

If you ask Thomson what was the most dangerous expedition he ever embarked on, he will probably reply, " Crossing Piccadilly." The finest thing that can be said of him is that during these four expeditions he never once fired a shot at a native. Other ex-

plorers have had to do so to save their
lives.   There were often occasions when
Thomson could have done it, to save his life
to all appearance, too.   The result of his
method of progressing is that where he has
gone—and he has been in parts of Africa
never before trod by the white man—he
really has "opened up the country" for those
who care to follow him.   Civilization by
bullet has only closed it elsewhere.   Yet
though there is an abundance of Scotch
caution about him, he is naturally an impul-
sive man, more inclined personally to march
straight on than to reach his destination by a
safer if more circuitous route.   Where only
his own life is concerned he gives you the
impression of one who might be rash, but his
prudence at the head of a caravan is at the
bottom of the faith that is placed in him.
According to a story that got into the papers
years ago, M. de Brazza once quarrelled with
Thomson in Africa, and all but struck him.
Thomson was praised for keeping his temper.
The story was a fabrication, but I fear that
if M. de Brazza had behaved like this,

Thomson would not have remembered to be diplomatic till some time afterwards. A truer tale might be told of an umbrella, gorgeous and wonderful to behold, that De Braza took to Africa to impress the natives with, and which Thomson subsequently presented to a dusky monarch.

The explorer has never shot a lion, though he has tracked a good many of them. Once he thought he had one. It was reclining in a little grove, and Thomson felt that it was his at last. With a trusty native he crept forward till he could obtain a good shot, and then fired. In breathless suspense he waited for its spring, and then when it did not spring he saw that he had shot it through the heart. However, it turned out only to be a large stone.

The young Scotchman sometimes thinks of the tremendous effect it would have had on the natives had he been the possessor of a complete set of artificial teeth. This is because he has one artificial tooth. Happening to take it out one day, an awe filled all who saw him, and from that hour he

was esteemed a medicine man. Another
excellent way of impressing Africa with the
grandeur of Britain was to take a photograph.
When the natives saw the camera aimed at
them they fell to the ground vanquished.

When Thomson was recently in this
country, he occasionally took a walk of
twenty or thirty miles to give him an appe-
tite for dinner. This he calls a stroll. One
day he strolled from Thornhill to Edinburgh,
had dinner, and then went to the Exhibition.
In appearance he is tall and strongly knit
rather than heavily built, and if you see him
more than once in the same week, you dis-
cover that he has still an interest in neck-
ties. Perhaps his most remarkable feat
consisted in taking a bottle of brandy into
the heart of Africa, and bringing it back
intact.

X.

ROBERT LOUIS STEVENSON.

SOME men of letters, not necessarily the greatest, have an indescribable charm to which we give our hearts. Thackeray is the young man's first love. Of living authors none perhaps bewitches the reader more than Mr. Stevenson, who plays upon words as if they were a musical instrument. To follow the music is less difficult than to place the musician. A friend of mine, who, like Mr. Grant Allen, reviews 365 books a year, and 366 in leap years, recently arranged the novelists of to-day in order of merit. Meredith, of course, he wrote first, and then there was a fall to Hardy. " Haggard," he explained, "I dropped from the Eiffel Tower; but what can I do with Stevenson ? I can't put him before ' Lorna Doone.' " So Mr. Stevenson puzzles the critics, fascinating them until they are willing to judge him by

7

the great work he is to write by and by
when the little books are finished. Over
"Treasure Island" I let my fire die in
winter without knowing that I was freezing.
But the creator of Alan Breck has now
published nearly twenty volumes. It is so
much easier to finish the little works than to
begin the great one, for which we are all
taking notes.

Mr. Stevenson is not to be labelled novelist. He wanders the byways of literature
without any fixed address. Too much of a
truant to be classified with the other boys,
he is only a writer of fiction in the sense that
he was once an Edinburgh University student because now and again he looked in at
his classes when he happened to be that way.
A literary man without a fixed occupation
amazes Mr. Henry James, a master in the
school of fiction which tells, in three volumes,
how Hiram K. Wilding trod on the skirt of
Alice M. Sparkins without anything's coming
of it. Mr. James analyzes Mr. Stevenson
with immense cleverness, but without sum-
ming up. That "Dr. Jekyll and Mr. Hyde"

should be by the author of "Treasure Island," "Virginibus Puerisque" by the author
of "The New Arabian Nights," "A Child's
Garden of Verses" by the author of "Prince
Otto," are to him the three degrees of com-
parison of wonder, though for my own part
I marvel more that the author of "Daisy
Miller" should be Mr. Stevenson's eulogist.
One conceives Mr. James a boy in velveteens
looking fearfully at Stevenson playing at
pirates.

There is nothing in Mr. Stevenson's sometimes writing essays, sometimes romances,
and anon poems to mark him versatile beyond other authors. One dreads his continuing
to do so, with so many books at his back, lest
it means weakness rather than strength. He
experiments too long; he is still a boy
wondering what he is going to be. With
Cowley's candour he tells us that he wants to
write something by which he may be for ever
known. His attempts in this direction have
been in the nature of trying different ways,
and he always starts off whistling. Having
gone so far without losing himself, he turns

back to try another road. Does his heart fail him, despite his jaunty bearing, or is it because there is no hurry? Though all his books are obviously by the same hand, no living writer has come so near fame from so many different sides. Where is the man among us who could write another "Virginibus Puerisque," the most delightful volume for the hammock ever sung in prose? The poems are as exquisite as they are artificial. "Jekyll and Hyde" is the greatest triumph extant in Christmas literature of the morbid kind. The donkey on the Cevennes (how Mr. Stevenson belaboured him!) only stands second to the "Inland Voyage." "Kidnapped" is the outstanding boy's book of its generation. "The Black Arrow" alone, to my thinking, is second-class. We shall all be doleful if a marksman who can pepper his target with inners does not reach the bull's-eye. But it is quite time the great work was begun. The sun sinks while the climber walks round his mountain, looking for the best way up.

Hard necessity has kept some great

writers from doing their best work, but Mr.
Stevenson is at last so firmly established that
if he continues to be versatile it will only
be from choice. He has attained a popularity such as is, as a rule, only accorded to
classic authors or to charlatans. For this he
has America to thank rather that Britain,
for the Americans buy his books, the only
honour a writer's admirers are slow to pay
him. Mr. Stevenson's reputation in the
United States is creditable to that country,
which has given him a position here in which
only a few saw him when he left. Unfor-
tunately, with popularity has come publicity.
All day the reporters sit on his garden wall.

No man has written in a finer spirit of the
profession of letters than Mr. Stevenson, but
this gossip vulgarizes it. The adulation of
the American public and of a little band of
clever literary dandies in London, great in
criticism, of whom he has become the darling,
has made Mr. Stevenson complacent, and he
always tended perhaps to be a thought too
fond of his velvet coat. There is danger in
the delight with which his every scrap is now

received. A few years ago, when he was his own severest and sanest critic, he stopped the publication of a book after it was in proof —a brave act. He has lost this courage, or or he would have re-written "The Black Arrow." There is deterioration in the essays he has been contributing to an American magazine, graceful and suggestive though they are. The most charming of living stylists, Mr. Stevenson is self-conscious in all his books now and again, but hitherto it has been the self-consciousness of an artist with severe critics at his shoulder. It has become self-satisfaction. The critics have put a giant's robe on him, and he has not flung it off. He dismisses "Tom Jones" with a simper. Personally Thackeray "scarce appeals to us as the ideal gentleman ; if there were nothing else [what else is there?], perpetual nosing after snobbery at least suggests the snob." From Mr. Stevenson one would not have expected the revival of this silly charge, which makes a cabbage of every man who writes about cabbages. I shall say no more of these ill-considered papers, though the sneers at Fielding call for indignant remonstrance, beyond expressing a hope that they lie buried between magazine covers. Mr. Stevenson has reached the critical point in his career, and one would like to see him back at Bournemouth, writing within high walls. We want that big book ; we think he is capable of it, and so we cannot afford to let him drift into the seaweed. About the writer with whom his name is so often absurdly linked we feel differently. It is as foolish to rail at Mr. Rider Haggard's complacency as it would be to blame Christopher Sly for so quickly believing that he was born a lord.

The key - note of all Mr. Stevenson's writings is his indifference, so far as his books are concerned, to the affairs of life and death on which other minds are chiefly set. Whether man has an immortal soul interests him as an artist not a whit : what is to come of man troubles him as little as where man came from. He is a warm, genial writer, yet this is so strange as to seem inhuman. His philosophy is that we

are but as the light-hearted birds. This is
our moment of being ; let us play the in-
toxicating game of life beautifully, artisti-
cally, before we fall dead from the tree.
We all know it is only in his books that Mr.
Stevenson can live this life. The cry is to
arms ; spears glisten in the sun ; see the
brave bark riding joyously on the waves, the
black flag, the dash of red colour twisting
round a mountainside. Alas ! the drummer
lies on a couch beating his drum. It is a
pathetic picture, less true to fact now, one
rejoices to know, that it was recently. A
common theory is that Mr. Stevenson dreams
an ideal life to escape from his own suffer-
ings. This sentimental plea suits very well.
The noticeable thing, however, is that the
grotesque, the uncanny, holds his soul ; his
brain will only follow a coloured clue. The
result is that he is chiefly picturesque, and, to
those who want more than art for art's sake,
never satisfying. Fascinating as his verses
are, artless in the perfection of art, they take
no reader a step forward. The children of
whom he sings so sweetly are cherubs without

souls.   It is not in poetry that Mr. Stevenson will give the great book to the world,
nor will it, I think, be in the form of essays.
Of late he has done nothing quite so fine as
" Virginibus Puerisque," though most of his
essays are gardens in which grow few weeds.
Quaint in matter as in treatment, they are
the best strictly literary essays of the day,
and their mixture of tenderness with humour
suggests Charles Lamb.   Some think Mr.
Stevenson's essays equal to Lamb's, or
greater.   To that I say No.   The name of
Lamb will for many a year bring proud tears
to English eyes.   Here was a man, weak like
the rest of us, who kept his sorrows to himself.   Life to him was not among the trees.
He had loved and lost.   Grief laid a heavy
hand on his brave brow.   Dark were his
nights ; horrid shadows in the house ; sudden
terrors ; the heart stops beating waiting for
a footstep.   At that door comes Tragedy,
knocking at all hours.   Was Lamb dis-
mayed ?   The tragedy of his life was not
drear to him.   It was wound round those
who were dearest to him ; it let him know

that life has a glory even at its saddest, that humour and pathos clasp hands, that loved ones are drawn nearer, and the soul strengthened in the presence of anguish, pain, and death. When Lamb sat down to write he did not pull down his blind on all that is greatest, if most awful, in human life. He was gentle, kindly; but he did not play at pretending that there is no cemetery round the corner. In Mr. Stevenson's exquisite essays one looks in vain for the great heart that palpitates through the pages of Charles Lamb.

The great work, if we are not to be disappointed, will be fiction. Mr. Stevenson is said to feel this himself, and, as I understand, "Harry Shovel" will be his biggest bid for fame. It is to be, broadly speaking, a nineteenth-century "Peregrine Pickle," dashed with Meredith, and this in the teeth of many admirers who maintain that the best of the author is Scottish. Mr. Stevenson, however, knows what he is about. Critics have said enthusiastically—for it is difficult to write of Mr. Stevenson without enthusiasm

—that Alan Breck is as good as anything in Scott. Alan Breck is certainly a masterpiece, quite worthy of the greatest of all storytellers, who, nevertheless, it should be remembered, created these rich side characters by the score, another before dinner-time. English critics have taken Alan to their hearts, and appreciate him thoroughly ; the reason, no doubt, being that he is the character whom England acknowledges as the Scottish type. The Highlands, which are Scotland to the same extent as Northumberland is England, present such a character to this day, but no deep knowledge of Mr. Stevenson's native country was required to reproduce him. An artistic Englishman or American could have done it. Scottish religion, I think, Mr. Stevenson has never understood, except as the outsider misunderstands it. He thinks it hard because there are no coloured windows. " The colour of Scotland has entered into him altogether," says Mr. James, who, we gather, conceives in Edinburgh Castle a a place where tartans glisten in the sun, while rocks re-echo bagpipes. Mr. James is right

in a way.   It is the tartan, the claymore, the
cry that the heather is on fire, that are Scotland to Mr. Stevenson.   But the Scotland
of our day is not a country rich in colour ; a
sombre grey prevails.   Thus, though Mr.
Stevenson's best romance is Scottish, that is
only, I think, because of his extraordinary
aptitude for the picturesque.   Give him any
period in any country that is romantic, and
he will soon steep himself in the kind of
knowledge he can best turn to account.
Adventures suit him best, the ladies being
left behind ; and so long as he is in fettle
it matters little whether the scene be Scotland or Spain.   The great thing is that
he should now give to one ambitious book
the time in which he has hitherto written
half a dozen small ones.   He will have to
take existence a little more seriously—to
weave broadcloth instead of lace.

XI

REV. WALTER C. SMITH, D.D.

DURING the four winters another and I were in Edinburgh we never entered any but Free churches. This seems to have been less on account of a scorn for other denominations than because we never thought of them. We felt sorry for the " men " who knew no better than to claim to be on the side of Dr. Macgregor. Even our Free kirks were limited to two, St. George's and the Free High. After all, we must have been liberally minded beyond most of our fellows, for, as a rule, those who frequented one of these churches shook their heads at the other. It is said that Dr. Whyte and Dr. Smith have a great appreciation of each other. They, too, are liberally minded.

To contrast the two leading Free Church ministers in Edinburgh as they struck a student would be to become a boy again.

The one is always ready to go on fire, and the other is sometimes at hand with a jug of cold water. Dr. Smith counts a hundred before he starts, whilst the minister of Free St. George's is off at once at a gallop, and would always arrive first at his destination if he had not sometimes to turn back. He is not only a Gladstonian, but Gladstonian; his enthusiasm carries him on as steam drives the engine. Dr. Smith being a critic, with a faculty of satire, what would rouse the one man makes the other smile. Dr. Whyte judges you as you are at the moment; Dr. Smith sees what you will be like to-morrow. Some years ago the defeated side in a great Assembly fight met at a breakfast to reason itself into a belief that it had gained a remarkable moral victory. Dr. Whyte and Dr. Smith were both present, and the former was so inspiriting that the breakfast became a scene of enthusiasm. Then Dr. Smith arose and made a remark about a company of Mark Tapleys—after which the meeting broke up.

I have a curious reminiscence of the

student who most frequently accompanied me to church in Edinburgh. One Sunday when we were on our way up slushy Bath Street to Free St. George's he discovered that he had not a penny for the plate. I suggested to him to give twopence next time; but no, he turned back to our lodgings for the penny. Sometime afterwards he found himself in the same position when we were nearing the Free High. " I'll give twopence next time," he said, cheerfully. I have thought this over since then, and wondered if there was anything in it.

The most glorious privilege of the old is to assist the young. The two ministers who are among the chief pillars of the Free Church in Edinburgh are not old yet, but they have had a long experience, and the strength and encouragement they have been to the young is the grand outstanding fact of their ministries. Their influence is, of course, chiefly noticeable in the divinity men, who make their Bible classes so remarkable. There is a sort of Freemasonry among the men who have come under the influence of

Dr. Smith. It seems to have steadied them
—to have given them wise rules of life that
have taken the noise out of them, and left
them undemonstrative, quiet, determined.
You will have little difficulty, as a rule, in
picking out Dr. Smith's men, whether in the
pulpit or in private. They have his mark,
as the Rugby boys were marked by Dr.
Arnold. Even in speaking of him, they
seldom talk in superlatives: only a light
comes into their eye, and you realize what a
well-founded reverence is. I met lately in
London an Irishman who, when the conversation turned to Scotland, asked what Edinburgh was doing without Dr. Smith (who
was in America at the time). He talked
with such obvious knowledge of Dr. Smith's
teaching, and with such affection for the man,
that by and by we were surprised to hear
that he had never heard him preach nor read
a line of his works. He explained that he
knew intimately two men who looked upon
their Sundays in the Free High, and still
more upon their private talks with the minister, as the turning point in their lives.

They were such fine fellows, and they were
so sure that they owed their development to
Dr. Smith, that to know the followers was to
know something of the master.   This it is to
be a touchstone to young men.

There are those who think Dr. Smith the
poet of higher account than Dr. Smith the
preacher.   I do not agree with them, though
there can be no question that the author of
" Olrig Grange " and Mr. Alexander Ander-
son are the two men now in Edinburgh who
have (at times) the divine afflatus.   " Surface-
man " is a true son of Burns.   Of him it may
be said, as it never can be said of Dr. Smith,
that he sings because he must.   His thoughts
run in harmonious numbers.   The author of
" Olrig Grange " is the stronger mind, however, and his lines are always pregnant of
meaning.   He is of the school of Mr. Lewis
Morris, but an immeasurably higher intellect
if not so fine an artist : indeed, though there
are hundreds of his pages that are not poetry,
there are almost none that could not be re-
written into weighty prose.   Sound is never
his sole object.   Good novels in verse are a

mistake, for it is quite certain they would be better in prose. The novelist has a great deal to say that cannot be said naturally in rhythm, and much of Dr. Smith's blank verse is good prose in frills. It is driven into an undeserved confinement.

The privilege of critics is to get twelve or twenty minor poets in a row, and then blow them all over at once. I remember one who dispatched Dr. Smith with a verse from the book under treatment. Dr. Smith writes of a poet's verses : " There is no sacred fire in them, Nor much of homely sense and shrewd," and when the critic came to these lines, he stopped reading : he declared that Dr. Smith had passed judgment on himself. This is a familiar form of criticism, but in the present case it had at least the demerit of being false. There is so much sacred fire about Dr. Smith's best poetry, that it is what makes him a poet ; and as for " homely sense and shrewd," he has simply more of it than any contemporary writer of verse. It is what gives heart to his satire, and keeps him from wounding merely for the pleasure of drawing blood. In conjunction with the sacred fire, the noble indignation that mean things should be, the insight into the tragic, it is what makes " Hilda " his greatest poem. Without it there could not be pathos, which is concerned with little things ; nor humour, nor, indeed, the flash into men and things that makes such a poem as " Dr. Linkletter's Scholar " as true as life, as sad as death. If only for the sake of that noble piece of writing, every Scottish student should have " North-Country Folk " in his possession. The poem is probably the most noteworthy thing that has been said of Northern University life.

UNWIN BROTHERS, PRINTERS, CHILWORTH AND LONDON.